PUFFIN BOOKS

ZOT'S TREASURES

When Zot the dog and his friend Clive go out looking for treasure, you can be sure not everything is what it seems. Zot's new hat looks very odd, and the jelly he finds in the pond is definitely *not* strawberry flavour. And what sort of monster could be making that terrifying noise?

Poor Mr Mole is rather annoyed when they start digging near his molehill, and horrid Mr Rat is very cross indeed when they beat him at his own game. But whatever they're doing, Zot and Clive always have plenty of fun!

Ivan Jones has been a teacher and Education Officer and is now a full-time writer. He contributes to various magazines, including *The Times Educational Supplement*, and is a regular broadcaster on Radio Shropshire. He lives in Shropshire and has three children.

Also by Ivan Jones

ADVENTURES OF ZOT THE DOG

Ivan Jones

Zot's Treasures

Illustrated by
Judy Brown

PUFFIN BOOKS

*To my parents,
my brother, Gerald,
and my sister, Diane*

PUFFIN BOOKS

Published by the Penguin Group
Penguin Books Ltd, 27 Wrights Lane, London W8 5TZ, England
Viking Penguin, a division of Penguin Books USA Inc.
375 Hudson Street, New York, New York 10014, USA
Penguin Books Australia Ltd, Ringwood, Victoria, Australia
Penguin Books Canada Ltd, 2801 John Street, Markham, Ontario, Canada L3R 1B4
Penguin Books (NZ) Ltd, 182–190 Wairau Road, Auckland 10, New Zealand

Penguin Books Ltd, Registered Offices: Harmondsworth, Middlesex, England

First published by Viking 1990
Published in Puffin Books 1991
10 9 8 7 6 5 4 3 2 1

Text copyright © Ivan Jones, 1990
Illustrations copyright © Judy Brown, 1990
All rights reserved

The moral right of the author has been asserted

Filmset in Times (Linotron 202)

Printed in England by Clays Ltd, St Ives plc

Except in the United States of America, this book is sold subject to
the condition that it shall not, by way of trade or otherwise, be lent,
re-sold, hired out, or otherwise circulated without the publisher's
prior consent in any form of binding or cover other than that in
which it is published and without a similar condition including this
condition being imposed on the subsequent purchaser

Contents

Zot and
the Treasure

In a little old house, down a little old lane, nearly hidden by trees and the humps of old pit mounds, live Zot the dog and his best friend, Clive.

One day, Zot and Clive went out hunting for treasure. They searched in the soft grass for gold. They fished in the pond for pearls. They dug in the mud for diamonds.

"I can smell something," said Zot. He put his nose to the ground and sniffed about until

he came to a hole.

"Woof!" he barked. "It's here!"

"What is?" Clive said.

"It might be a rabbit," said Zot.

"Rabbit?" Clive scratched his head. "That *is* a kind of treasure, I suppose."

Zot began to dig furiously. He
flung out something squidgy and
squirmy. It slapped into Clive's
face.

"Ugh!" cried Clive. "What was that?"

It wriggled on the floor.

"Worms!" Zot woofed. "Lots and lots of worms."

"What do you think you're doing?" gasped a cross voice. "That's my larder you're digging up."

It was Mr Mole. His head poked out of a molehill behind them.

"Woof," said Zot. "We're looking for treasure."

Mr Mole shuffled forwards and began shovelling the earth back over his worms.

"More like digging up my worm larder!" he muttered.

"It was a mistake," said Clive.

"Don't you eat worms?"
asked Mr Mole, looking
puzzled.

"No," said Clive. "We don't!"

Zot shook his head. Mr Mole
squinted.

"I don't know how you can
stand this daylight," he winced,
and climbed back into his
molehill.

"By the way," he said, looking over his shoulder, "do you like elephant eggs?"

Zot woofed.

"There's one over there." Mr Mole pointed to the foot of a tree. Then he popped back into his dark hole.

"What do you think?" asked Clive.

"It can't be worse than worms," Zot said. He dashed to the tree and started sniffing.

Clive searched among the leaves. "I've found something!" he cried.

"Is it smooth and shiny?" Zot asked.

"Dull," Clive said, "and wrinkled . . ."

"Is it gold?" Zot squealed.

"No," Clive said. "It's brown."

"Is it a jewel?"

"No," said Clive. "It's twitching."

"Twitching," said Zot. "Oh, then it MUST be the elephant's egg!"

"Let's take it home," said Clive.

"Put it in a jar," Zot woofed, "and see what happens."

They put the treasure in a jar and went to bed.

Later that night, Zot went to look at the elephant egg.

"Woof, woof!" he cried.

Clive ran downstairs. "What's the matter, Zot?"

"That egg's hatched into a pink elephant!" said Zot.

Clive grinned. "That's a

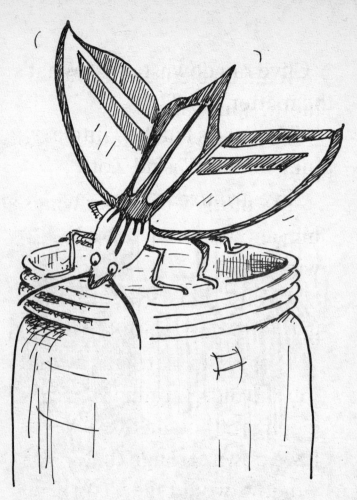

moth!" he said. "Elephants are much bigger."

The moth perched on the edge of the jar and stretched her wings.

"I am an elephant hawk-moth," she whispered.

"You are *very* beautiful," Zot said.

The moth winked her wings at him and fluttered out of the window.

"Well," said Clive, "that was good treasure, wasn't it?"

"Yes," said Zot. "It's a good job she didn't turn into a *real* elephant, though. She'd never have flown through that window, would she?"

Zot and Clive
at the Tip

Up at the tip, Zot saw a furry
thing sticking out of the ground.
"Woof!" he cried. "What's
this?"

21

"It could be a tail," Clive said.
Zot jumped on it and pulled it
with his teeth. He growled and

tugged at it, but it didn't budge.
"Let's dig it out," Zot said,
scrabbling with his paws.

Clive found an old spade so
that he could help him. They
dug and dug and dug.

"Is it a bone?" Zot woofed.

"No," said Clive, "it's a funny
old hat." He put it on his head
and grinned.

"I like hats," woofed Zot.
"Are there any more?"

"There's something here!"
Clive pointed. "It might be a
hat!"

They dug and dug and dug.

"It's a saucepan!" Clive
yelled.

"No," Zot woofed. "Not a

saucepan. It's a hat with a tail!"

Clive laughed and pushed the saucepan on to Zot's head. It slipped over his eyes.

"I like it," said Zot. "But I

can only see my feet!"

He and Clive jumped up and
down. Clive shouted
"Woopee!" and Zot barked
"Woofee!" Then Clive said,
"Let me try the hat with a tail."

"All right," said Zot. "Ouch!"

"What's the matter?" Clive said.

"It's stuck!" Zot groaned.

Clive pulled at the handle and pushed at the rim of the saucepan. But would it come off?

NO, IT WOULD NOT!

"I'm going to pot!" said Zot with a grin. "I don't want to be a dog with two tails."

"We'd better go home and try some butter," said Clive.

"Ugh!" woofed Zot.

"Or soap," said Clive. "Lots of soap all round your ears."

"UGH!" woofed Zot. He sat down and started to whine.

Master Rat hopped out of an old tin and looked at Zot and Clive. He put on a pair of old wire spectacles.

"What's up?" he said.

Clive pointed at the saucepan.

Master Rat smirked. "What's under it?" he said. "Is it a sheep?"

Zot woofed crossly.

"Well," said Rat, "if I were you I'd try a hammer. Hammer it off! Bang, bang, bang!"

"No, thank you," Zot protested. "I don't want a headache."

"Well," said Master Rat, "now, let me see. There was a case once where they used the slime of a slug to slip off a ring . . ."

"NO, THANK YOU!" Zot shouted.

"Or you might try rubbing

cuckoo spit round the edge . . ."
Rat chuckled.

"Never mind," quipped
Master Rat. "You probably look
better like that. You've heard of
a sausage dog; well, you're a
saucepan dog! Ha, ha, ha!"

"Woof!" Zot yapped. "And
you can be a tail-less rat!"

Master Rat dropped his
spectacles and ran. Zot sprang
at him, tripped over Rat's tin,
tumbled down a slope, bumped
into a tree and BANG!

The saucepan flew through
the air and landed . . .

**RIGHT ON TOP OF
MASTER RAT!**

"Drat!" Master Rat said.
"Drat! Drat! Drat!"

"Phew!" sighed Zot. "Thank
goodness that's off."

"Let me out!" squeaked
Master Rat. "It's horrible being
stuck in a pan."

"Yes," said Zot, "I know how you feel."

"Let me out!" screeched Master Rat.

Zot turned to Clive. Clive winked.

"Shall we hammer it, Zot?" he said. "Bang, bang, bang!"

"No!" squeaked Master Rat.

"Or we could try the slime of a slug," Clive went on. "There

was a case once where . . ."

"Please!" cried Rat.

Zot lifted the saucepan and Master Rat scurried away over the tip.

"Don't you want your specs?" Zot called after him.

"No!" gasped Master Rat.

"You need them more than me!"

"Cheek!" said Clive.

Suddenly Zot spotted an old boot. "Look," he said, "here's my new hat."

"Hat?" said Clive. Zot put his head in the boot.

"*Hat?*" Clive stared.

"Yes," Zot woofed. "It's bootiful!" And he bounced off home.

Zot and
the Jelly

One afternoon, Zot found
some jelly.

"Woof," he said. "Jelly for
tea!" He ran to the house to tell
Clive. Clive was making a kite.

"Mmm," he said, licking his
lips. "I love jelly!"

So Zot grabbed his bowl and
bolted down the lane.

"Is it strawberry jelly?" Clive

shouted after him. "Or
pineapple?"

But Zot didn't answer.

He didn't stop until he
reached the pond. He flopped

down at its edge. He sniffed at
the water. The big blob of gooey
jelly stuff had little black specks
all over it.

"Woof," he said. "I think it
must be blackcurrant jelly!"

Zot stretched forwards and

scooped up the jelly very
carefully on his long, pink
tongue. It wobbled and
shivered; it dribbled and tickled.

He flicked it into the bowl.

Mrs Frog popped out of the
water.

"What *are* you doing?" she demanded crossly.

"Er, nothing much," Zot said. "Just catching jelly."

Mrs Frog hopped on to the bank and peered into the bowl.

"Eek!" she cried. "That's my frogspawn. Put it back at once!"

"But I wanted it for tea," Zot woofed.

"Put it back!" croaked Mrs Frog. "It's mine!"

Zot tipped the jelly back into the pond. "Is it only for frogs to eat?" he said.

"Eat?" cried Mrs Frog. "We don't eat it! We *lay* it!"

"It must be very nice to be
able to lay it," said Zot. "Er,
what do you *do* with it . . . if
you don't eat it?"

"Do with it?" honked Mrs
Frog. "What do you *think* we do

with it? We just leave it until it hatches."

Zot stared. Mrs Frog swam away.

Zot wandered back to Clive.

"Where's the jelly?" Clive asked.

"It was Mrs Frog's," said Zot. "She told me to put it back in the pond."

Clive scratched his head.
"In the pond?" he said.
"What flavour was it?"

"Frogspawn flavour. But the frogs won't eat it," said Zot.

Clive began to laugh. "No," he said, "and I don't think I would either."

"She said it hatches," Zot woofed.

"It does," said Clive. "Those little black dots hatch into tadpoles. Then the tadpoles turn into frogs."

"What do frogs turn into?" asked Zot.

"Princes, I think," Clive said, with a chuckle.

"It's time for tea," said Clive.

"There isn't any jelly, is there?" woofed Zot.

"No," said Clive. "There's no jelly."

"Thank goodness for that," said Zot. "I wouldn't want a load of frogs wobbling about in my tummy . . ."

Would you?

Zot and
Master Rat

At the edge of the wood, Zot found a bone.

"Yum," he said. "This is my lucky day!"

He threw it up in the air and caught it. He flung it across the lane and pounced on it. And then he settled down on the ground to gnaw at it. He was very happy.

Master Rat came sniffing around.

"That sort of bone is very bad for you, you know," he said.

"Bad?" Zot woofed.

"Eating bones like that can cause very bad tummy-ache," said Rat with a sly smile.

"Woof," Zot said. "I *never* get tummy-ache. Never!"

And he went on munching at the bone.

"Ah!" Rat wheedled. "But that kind of bone can be very bad for your teeth as well. It's the sort of bone which gives you toothache."

"I wouldn't like toothache,"

woofed Zot. But he still went on crunching at the bone.

"Stop!" cried Master Rat. "There was a case where a bone like that gave a dog splinters in the throat. It made him very ill."

Zot growled at the bone.

"I'm not feeling so hungry

any more," he said miserably.

Master Rat sat up and stroked his whiskers.

Zot began to dig a hole next to the elder tree.

Clive came along. "Hello," he said. "What's this?"

Zot showed him the half-eaten bone.

"I'm burying it," he said.

"This kind of bone can give you
splinters and toothache and
tummy-ache . . ."

Clive frowned.

"Master Rat said so," said
Zot.

"Oh, I *see*," said Clive, "I
see." He scratched his ear

thoughtfully. "By the way, has anyone found any eggs?" he said.

"Eggs?" cried Master Rat, who loved eating eggs more than anything.

"Yes," said Clive. "Mrs Hen has been laying away and she

can't remember where she's left them."

He peeked at Rat out of the corner of his eye. Zot shook his head.

"Er, well," said Master Rat, "I'd better be going . . ." And he scurried away down the lane muttering, "Eggs! Eggs! I do *love* eggs!"

"Now for some fun!" Clive said.

He whispered something in Zot's ear. Zot wagged his tail and laughed. Then he and Clive filled in the hole next to the elder tree and hid behind some bushes.

Soon Master Rat came
hurrying back. He was very
cross.

"Eggs!" he said. "There
weren't no perishin' eggs! But at
least I'll have Zot's bone," he
cackled.

He began to dig. He made a

deep hole, but there was no
bone.

"Where is the pesky thing?"
he squeaked.

Zot and Clive strolled over.

Dirt was flying everywhere.

"Looking for something?" asked Clive.

"Oh, it's you," panted Master Rat. "I was just taking a bit of exercise."

"That *was* my bone hole!" Zot woofed.

"Was it?" squeaked Rat.

"Yes," Zot replied, grinning. "It's a good job I've eaten my bone after all, isn't it?"

"Eaten it?" Rat glared into the gloomy depths of the hole.

"Yes," woofed Zot. "Thank goodness I didn't bury it."

"Why?" asked Master Rat crossly.

"Well," Zot woofed, "you
might have dug it up and
thought it was yours!"

"Yes," said Clive. "And if
you'd eaten it, just think how
bad it would have been for your
tummy and teeth!"

"Not to mention your
throat!" woofed Zot.

"Mmm," said Clive. "It looks as if you and Zot have *both* had a lucky day."

"Drat!" said Rat angrily. "Drat, drat, drat!"

And he scurried off back to the tip.

"How are you feeling?" Clive said.

"Perfect!" Zot replied.

"No pains? No aches? No splinters in the throat?"

"No," Zot said, laughing, "but my sides are aching a bit."

Zot and
the Monster

Down by the pond, Zot heard
a strange noise. He pricked up
his ears.

"Woof!" he said. "What's
that?"

Fuffle! Fuffle! Flap! it went.

"Woof!" Zot squeaked. "It

67

might be a monster!"

There was a long *hissssss*
from the reeds.

"It *sounds* like a monster!"
said Zot, trembling.

FUFFLE! FLAP! FUFFLE!
"It *is* a MONSTER!" Zot
whimpered and ran off down
the lane.

"What's the matter?" asked Clive.

"There's a monster by the pond!" cried Zot.

Clive grinned.

"Don't be silly," he said. "You're barking up the wrong tree."

"I know a monster when I see one," Zot said.

"Have you *seen* it?" asked Clive.

"No," Zot admitted, "but I've heard it."

"It wasn't Mrs Frog by any chance?" asked Clive.

"No," said Zot, "it wasn't."

"Come with me," Clive said.

He and Zot crept back to the pond. They sneaked through the reeds and peeped through the stalks.

"Perhaps it's gone," whispered Zot.

"*Hisssssss!*" said a voice. "*Hissss hiss hissss!*"

Zot looked at Clive. Clive stared at Zot.

"It might EAT us!" said Zot.

They both jumped up with a howl and banged into each other. Clive fled down the lane. But Zot rolled through the reeds and bumped right into . . .

A BEAUTIFUL SWAN!

She was lying on her side,
whimpering, "Help me . . . help
me, please."

When she tried to get up, her

wings beat the reeds with a
Fuffle! Fuffle! Flap!
  Then she hissed angrily and
sank back on to the ground. She
was very tired.

"Well," said Zot, "you're a funny monster!"

The swan dipped her beautiful neck and flashed her beautiful eyes.

"Are you hurt?" Zot woofed.

The swan showed Zot her leg, all wrapped and trapped in fishing-line.

"I could try these," said Zot, showing her his sharp teeth.

The swan lifted her wing. Zot nibbled at the fishing-line. He gnawed and gnawed until all the loops were bitten through. The swan was free!

She stretched her leg and flapped her wings.

"Beautiful," Zot said
dreamily. "I wish I could fly!"
The swan wound her long neck
around Zot's neck and gave him

a little peck, like a kiss.

"You are very kind," she
whispered. Then she flapped
her strong wings again, and flew
away over the wood.

Then Zot heard a loud noise.
BANG! BANG! BANG! He
looked out of the reeds.

Clive was coming back with a
big, old tin drum to frighten
away the monster.

"Zot," he shouted, "are you

all right? I've come to rescue
you."

"It's gone now," Zot said. "It
was a *terrible* monster!"

"Was it BIG?" Clive
shrieked.

"Yes," Zot woofed, "but I
drove it away! And saved a
beautiful swan from its *terrible*
grip!"

Zot wagged his tail.

"A swan?" Clive said, putting
down the drum.

"Yes," said Zot, and ran
round in circles. "A *beautiful*
swan."

"Why are you running round
in circles?" said Clive.

"She kissed me," Zot woofed,
and bounced off home.

"Well I never," said Clive,
scratching his head. "It must be
puppy love!"